Jane Austen

HER COMPLETE NOVELS IN ONE SITTING

By Jennifer Kasius

RUNNING PRESS
PHILADELPHIA · LONDON

A Running Press® Miniature Edition™
© 2012 by Running Press
All rights reserved under the Pan-American and International
Copyright Conventions
Printed in China

9 8 7 6 5 4 3 2 1

Digit on the right indicates the number of this printing

Library of Congress Control Number: 2012938300

ISBN 978-0-7624-4755-8

Running Press Book Publishers
A Member of the Perseus Books Group
2300 Chestnut Street
Philadelphia, PA 19103-4371

Visit us on the web!
www.runningpress.com

Contents

Introduction

IT IS A TRUTH UNIVERSALLY acknowledged that Jane Austen is one of the greatest writers in the English literary canon—as well as an unlikely pop-culture icon. If Jane Austen visited us in a time machine, would she be surprised at the fervor of today's "Janeites," or be

astounded that her storylines
have inspired spin-offs like
Bridget Jones' Diary, Clueless,
and even (gasp) *Pride and
Prejudice and Zombies*?
Could spinster Jane fathom
that there would be dating
guides that use her novels as
tools for solving modern-day
relationship struggles?
Would she swoon over Colin
Firth's portrayal of Darcy, or

Life of
Jane Austen

JANE AUSTEN WAS BORN ON
December 16, 1775 in the parsonage at Stevenson, Hamp-
shire. She was a clergyman's
daughter, the seventh of eight
children. By all accounts she
had a pleasant childhood,
brought up in a home in which

she was surrounded by books. She and her sister Cassandra went to boarding school for a time, but most of her education was accomplished at home. She began to write; at first to amuse her family, then in earnest when she was twenty-one years old and began writing a novel entitled *First Impressions* (which would later become *Pride and Prejudice*). Her father approached a publisher on her behalf, but the manuscript was rejected. She continued to write, and by the late 1790s she had created early versions of *Northanger Abbey* and *Sense and Sensibility* (at first titled *Elinor and Marianne*).

In 1801, her father moved the family to the resort town of Bath, a place that she apparently loathed. She allegedly had a romance with a young clergyman, but tragically he died before there was a marriage proposal. Jane was later engaged to a friend, Harris Bigg-Wither, but she broke it off after just a day—most likely realizing they were not compatible. At the time she was twenty-seven (perhaps tellingly, the same age as her protagonist Anne Elliot in *Persuasion*). There is no record of any romantic attachments during Jane's lifetime following that short-lived engagement.

Jane's father died in 1805, which left her and her mother and sister with a greatly reduced income (not unlike the Dashwoods in *Sense and Sensibility*). Her landowner brother Edward provided them a cottage in the peaceful town of Chawton, a place where Jane settled very happily and enjoyed the most productive period of her life. She went back to the early versions of her novels and finished them. *Sense and Sensibility* was the first to appear in 1811 (credited as "By a Lady"), followed by *Pride and Prejudice* in 1813. *Mansfield Park* was published in 1814 and *Emma* in 1816. She began work on *Persuasion* in

1816 and completed it in 1817, while her health was failing. She then started (but never finished) a work called *Sandition*. Jane Austen died on July 18, 1817, at the age of forty-one. Both *Persuasion* and *Northanger Abbey* (a work which, curiously, had been bought by a publisher but shelved for years) were published posthumously in 1818.

Since then, Jane Austen's
novels have never fallen out
of print.

Sense and Sensibility

(1811)

"[Elinor] had an excellent
heart—her disposition was
affectionate, and her feelings were
strong; but she knew how
to govern them; it was a

*knowledge which her mother had
yet to learn, and which
one of her sisters had resolved
never to be taught."*

MAJOR CHARACTERS

Elinor Dashwood: The eldest of
the Dashwood sisters and heroine of the novel, whose tempera-

ment is cautious, prudent, calm, and reserved.

Marianne Dashwood: Elinor's younger sister, her nature is impulsive, passionate, and forthright.

Mrs. Dashwood: Widowed at the start of the novel, Elinor and Marianne's mother is at the financial mercy of her husband's son.

John Dashwood: The heir of the Dashwood estate—a weak-minded man who is too easily influenced by his greedy wife.

Sir John Middleton: A distant relative who offers the Dashwood ladies both a new home and a new social circle.

Colonel Brandon: A bachelor who is considered generally

quiet (and in Marianne's estimation, boring)—but he is strong and reliable in a crisis.

Edward Ferrars: The firstborn son of a high-minded family—he is expected to make a prosperous living, as well as a prosperous marriage.

Lucy Steele: A young lady who reveals herself to be intellectually dim—but calculating in character.

John Willoughby: An attractive, captivating gentleman who inspires strong feelings in Marianne.

The Story

Mr. Henry Dashwood dies, leaving his estate and money to his son from his first marriage,

John. At his father's deathbed,
John Dashwood promises that
he will do everything in his
power to provide for Henry's
widow and daughters. But his
idea of what is meant by "pro-
viding for" diminishes at the
influence of his wife, Fanny,
who convinces him that his
promise means nothing more
than to send his stepmother
and half-sisters "occasional

presents of fish and game, when they are in season." Because of Fanny's powers of persuasion (as well as the laws that prevented females from inheriting estates) Mrs. Dashwood and her daughters, Elinor, Marianne, and little Margaret, are turned out of their home and left with a mere pittance. Fortuitously, a distant relative, Sir John Middleton, invites them to rent out a small but charming cottage on his estate. They are happily settled at Barton Cottage, and the affable Sir John introduces the Dashwood ladies to his connections, including his mother-in-law Mrs. Jennings and his friend Colonel Brandon.

One day while strolling in the countryside, Marianne twists her ankle. A handsome stranger appears and carries her back home, promising to look in on her the next day. This dashing young man is John Willoughby, who is visiting a nearby relation. He proves to be charming in every way: kind, engaging, witty, and clearly smitten with Marianne. In turn, Marianne throws herself headlong into what seems to be a happy attachment—

even when it means engaging in mildly imprudent actions: for example, Willoughby tries to give Marianne a horse; an extravagant, impractical present she can't accept. Later, the two make an (unaccompanied) visit to the home he is expected to inherit—a clear indication to Marianne that she will soon be Mrs. Willoughby.

Everyone is genuinely

pleased to see the mutual devotion developing between the two. Everyone that is, except for Colonel Brandon. The colonel admires Marianne from afar, but Marianne only has eyes for Willoughby. Governed by "sensibility," Marianne expresses her love passionately, openly, and with abandon.

Meanwhile, Elinor is harboring an attachment of her own,

but unlike her sister, she keeps her feelings to herself. While she was still at the Dashwood estate, Elinor had spent some time with Edward Ferrars (brother to the odious Fanny). As the eldest son of a wealthy family, Edward is expected to enter a profession that will give him "a fine figure" in the world. Yet, he wishes only to lead a quiet life and become a clergyman.

Fanny had observed the growing attachment between her brother and Elinor, and commented to Mrs. Dashwood that the marriage would be beneath her brother's station: a remark that incited Mrs. Dashwood to hasten their family's departure. Since then, Elinor has pined for her secret love, but guided by "sense," she is guarded with her emotions until she can be sure that they are reciprocated.

Quite unexpectedly, Willoughby is called away to London, and offers no immediate promise of his return. Marianne is grieved by his sudden departure, but trusts that he'll soon provide a good reason for his odd behavior. Marianne's hopes for his return are roused when she sees a man riding toward the cottage—yet it is not Willoughby, but rather Edward, coming for a visit. Elinor observes that Edward is in low spirits, somewhat distant, often lost in thought. The only indication that he may still have feelings for Elinor rests on his finger, in the form of a ring that contains a lock of her hair. He departs, looking more despondent and morose than when he arrived.

Elinor and Marianne are
introduced to the Steele sisters,
young ladies who are distant
relations of Mrs. Jennings.
Lucy Steele quickly takes Elinor into her confidence: Lucy
reveals that she has been
secretly engaged to Edward for
four years, but since Edward's
mother would never approve
the match, he risks being disin-
herited. Elinor notices that

Lucy's shade of hair is the same as her own, and thus realizes her mistaken assumption regarding Edward's ring. With great composure, she listens to Lucy's tale, even though her hopes for love are dashed. At the same time, she feels badly for Edward for promising himself to Lucy, who is not his equal in intellect or character. Elinor decides to keep Lucy's admission a secret from her mother and Marianne, and bears her pain in private.

Mrs. Jennings invites the Dashwood sisters to accompany her to her London home. As soon as they arrive, Marianne sends a note to Willoughby, hoping for him to come immediately. She grows increasingly melancholy over his silence as the days go by. They attend a ball, and finally encounter Willoughby, who icily rebuffs Marianne. He later sends her a formal letter to say he is sorry if she presumed there was anything more than friendship between them. Marianne is inconsolable, and takes to her bed for several days, unable to eat or sleep.

Hearing of Marianne's distress, Colonel Brandon then relates his own sad story to Eli-

nor, which enlightens her to
Willoughby's true nature. Many
years ago, the colonel was
deeply in love with his childhood sweetheart, but she was
married off to Brandon's older
brother, who treated her cruelly. As a result, she descended
into a life of scandal and
debauchery. Brandon eventually
discovered his old love in a poor-
house, on the edge of death, with

an illegitimate infant. Brandon
had taken his beloved's daughter,
Eliza, and provided for her. As
cruel fate would have it, years
later, Eliza was seduced by none
other than ... Willoughby. Brandon found Eliza abandoned and
expecting Willoughby's child.
The scandal was never made
public—and Willoughby is now
desperate to support his spend-
thrift lifestyle by marrying the

very wealthy Sophia Grey. Elinor resolves to inform Marianne of this astonishing tale once her sister is well enough.

News of Lucy and Edward's engagement has inadvertently been revealed, and Mrs. Ferrars, as predicted, disinherits her son because of the unsuitable match. The Ferrars money will now go to Edward's younger brother, Robert. Elinor hears that Edward is still intent on marrying Lucy, despite his change in fortune. Eager to leave London, Elinor and Marianne depart for their friends' estate at Somersetshire, where they will stay for a few days before they continue their journey home.

While at Somersetshire, Marianne falls gravely ill, delirious with fever. Brandon sets off to fetch Mrs. Dashwood as soon as possible—so she can be by her daughter's side in case the worst happens. Hearing that Marianne may be at death's door, a contrite Willoughby pays a visit. He endeavors to explain to Elinor the reasons for his behavior. He admits that at first, his overtures toward Marianne were only a passing fancy, but then his regard for her deepened, saying that "the happiest hours of my life were with her." But he was torn—because he knew his own fallible nature, and that he must attach himself to a woman of fortune. Then an event occurred that forced his decision: his rich aunt discovered his indiscretion with Eliza, and insisted that he marry her. He refused her request, and resolved to flee to London in pursuit of Ms. Grey, a connection that would once and for all secure his financial position. Yet he has never forgotten Marianne, and lives with a sense of regret for what is ultimately lost between them.

Much to the relief of everyone, Marianne recovers, and Elinor eventually tells her Willoughby's story. Marianne sees clearly that her "sensibility" led her to love Willoughby without restraint—

and they could never have been happy together.

The sisters are back home at Barton when Edward unexpectedly arrives. They all assume that he is already married to Lucy, and they inquire about "Mrs. Ferrars." After some initial awkwardness and confusion, Edward delivers the incredible news that Lucy is now married to his brother, Robert. Apparently Lucy's affections transferred to the brother who is now in possession of the family fortune. Upon hearing that Edward is free from his engagement, Elinor forgets her "sense" and is overcome with emotion. Edward immediately proposes to her, saying that he has been wallowing in misery over his bounden duty to Lucy. Happily, Mrs. Ferrars gives up her notion of completely disinheriting Edward, and the couple will now have enough money to live on—and Edward can pursue his position as a curate on Brandon's estate. Meanwhile, Marianne comes to see that Colonel Brandon is an exemplary man who genuinely loves her. The two sisters both settle into blissful marriages, living "within sight of one another" and living "without disagree-

ment between themselves."
Sense and Sensibility now find a
happy equilibrium.

Pride
and
Prejudice

(1813)

*"It is a truth universally ack-
nowledged that a single man
in possession of a good fortune
must be in want of a wife."*

~~~~~
MAJOR CHARACTERS

Elizabeth Bennet: A gentle-woman who is the second of the five Bennet daughters. The novel's protagonist, she is the sharpest of mind—and often the sharpest in tongue.

Mr. Fitzwilliam Darcy: Master of the grand estate of Pemberley and in possession of "ten thousand a year." He is perceived to have an air of arrogance.

Charles Bingley: Good friend to Mr. Darcy and new tenant of the Netherfield estate.

Jane Bennet: The eldest of the Bennet daughters—and known

to be the most beautiful and
sweet-tempered.

Mr. and Mrs. Gardiner:
Elizabeth and Jane's beloved
aunt and uncle, who display
good sense and fortitude.

Mr. George Wickham: An army
officer stationed at the nearby
village of Meryton. He claims to

have well-founded grudges
against Mr. Darcy.

Mr. Collins: Elizabeth's inane
and vainglorious cousin, he is
also heir to the Bennet estate.

Lydia Bennet: The "very silly"
and youngest Bennet daughter,
her favorite pastime is shamelessly flirting with army officers.

THE STORY

With the famous first line, "It is a truth universally acknowledged that a single man in possession of a good fortune must be in want of a wife," Austen launches her most well-known and perhaps most beloved novel. It is the story of Elizabeth Bennet, the second of the five Bennet daughters. She and her older sister Jane are generally thought to be the most sensible members of their family. Her mother and younger sisters too often display foolish behavior—but Elizabeth and Jane do their best not to have the family's conduct reflect on their own reputations. Upon hearing that the nearby estate of Netherfield is to be rented to a wealthy young man, Charles Bingley, Mrs. Bennet is deter-

mined that one of her daughters
will captivate the newcomer.
The chance for a meeting comes
at the village ball, where the
Bennets also meet Mr. Bingley's
sisters and his close friend, Mr.
Fitzwilliam Darcy, who is dis-
dainful of the small country
gathering. When it is suggested
that Mr. Darcy ask Elizabeth to
dance with him, she overhears
him remarking, "She is tolera-

ble, but not handsome enough
to tempt me." So goes the disastrous first impressions between
Elizabeth Bennet and Mr. Darcy.

Happily, there is one star-
crossed connection at the ball,
and that is between Jane and
Mr. Bingley. Soon Jane is
invited by Bingley's sisters to
dine at Netherfield. Crafty Mrs.
Bennet insists that Jane make
the three-mile journey by

horseback instead of by carriage, hoping that the rain will extend her stay. Indeed, Jane comes down with a bad cold, and must recover at Netherfield for several days. Elizabeth visits her ailing sister, which gives her the opportunity to spend more time with the Bingleys and Mr. Darcy. While Mr. Bingley is extremely good-natured, Elizabeth's prior judgment of the rest of the party stands firm. The Bingley sisters are snobbish and self-important, and Darcy is ill-tempered and proud.

When Elizabeth and Jane return home, they discover that their estranged cousin, Mr. Collins, will be making an unexpected visit. Mr. Collins is a buffoon and a blowhard, who repeatedly boasts of his association with his esteemed patroness, the Lady Catherine de Bourgh, who has given Mr. Collins a post as a clergyman on her estate of Rosings. Strongly opinionated, Lady Catherine has also made it clear that a man of Mr. Collins' position must secure a wife. Because Mr. Collins will eventually inherit the Bennet estate (since Mr. Bennet has no male heir), he congratulates himself for being so charitable as to choose a wife from among Mr. Bennet's daughters. He sets his sights on Elizabeth, assuring her of the "violence of his affection" and making a most awkward proposal of marriage. Elizabeth refuses, to the great distress of her mother. But Mr. Collins soon recovers from his rejection—and a few days later he is engaged to Elizabeth's good friend, Charlotte Lucas. Elizabeth is upset that Charlotte should accept such a foolish man, but Charlotte assures her, "I am not romantic . . . I ask only a comfortable home." Charlotte is an unmarried woman without fortune, and sees Mr. Collins as her best hope of living a good life.

Meanwhile, Elizabeth makes

the acquaintance of a charming
army officer, Mr. Wickham,
who tells her of his sad history
with the Darcy family. Mr.
Wickham had grown up on the
Darcy estate of Pemberley: Mr.
Darcy's father had treated him
like a godson, and meant to
secure a position for Wickham
in the church. But upon the
elder Mr. Darcy's death, his son
had cheated Wickham out of

his rightful inheritance, which forced Wickham to enter the militia to support himself. This scandalous story further cements Elizabeth's bad opinion of Darcy—thinking him now not just proud, but outright dishonest.

Jane gets a surprising letter from Mr. Bingley's sister, saying that the entire Netherfield party has packed up and gone to London for the winter. Jane is shocked and saddened at their sudden departure—most of all because Bingley left without saying goodbye. But she bears it stoically, always ready to believe the best of everyone. Fortuitously, Jane gets an offer from her uncle and aunt to stay at their London home. Jane hopes for a visit from Mr. Bingley during the several months

that she is with the Gardiners,
but he never appears. She can
only conclude that he never
truly cared for her.

Charlotte begs Elizabeth to
visit her new married home at
the Rosings estate, which gives
Elizabeth the opportunity to
meet the imposing Lady
Catherine de Bourgh, who also
happens to be Mr. Darcy's aunt.
Elizabeth and Mr. Darcy meet

several times during her time at Rosings, and the two resume their verbal sparring. She also meets Mr. Darcy's cousin, Colonel Fitzwilliam, who inadvertently reveals that Darcy has recently saved his friend Bingley from a most unsuitable match. This gives Elizabeth yet another reason to despise Darcy—he is the influence behind Bingley's departure from Netherfield, and the source of Jane's unhappiness.

Elizabeth is stunned when
Mr. Darcy tells her, "In vain I
have struggled . . . You must
allow me to tell you how
ardently I admire and love you."
Elizabeth coolly and angrily
asks him why "you chose to tell
me that you like me against
your will, against your reason,
and even against your character." She then levels every

charge against him: recounting his injustice to Wickham and his role in impeding the romance between Jane and Bingley. She clinches her speech by saying that from the first moment of meeting him, she had the "fullest belief of your arrogance, your conceit, and your selfish disdain of the feelings of others."

Darcy departs, but the next

morning delivers a long letter, which informs Elizabeth where she has been correct in her estimation of his behavior—and where she has been sorely misled. He admits that he discouraged Bingley, partly because he doubted Jane's affection for his friend but also because of the impropriety displayed by other members of the Bennet family. Indeed, Elizabeth is mortified to recall some of her younger sisters' behavior, particularly at the Netherfield Ball—and is forced to admit to herself that their conduct would make some suitors reluctant to be connected to such a foolish family.

She continues reading the letter, where he refutes the charge of having injured Mr. Wickham—the true account is that Mr. Darcy had endeavored to find him a suitable position in the church, but Wickham squandered this opportunity, as well his rightful inherited sum, with his life of debauchery. When Darcy refused to bequeath him any more money, Wickham took revenge by attempting to elope with Darcy's beloved younger sister Georgiana. Luckily, Wickham's wicked plan to get to Geor-

giana's fortune was thwarted at
the eleventh hour. Wanting to
protect his sister from possible
disgrace, Mr. Darcy has not pub-
licized Wickham's true nature.
Upon reading this account, Elizabeth chooses to honor Mr.
Darcy's privacy and relate the
letter's content only to Jane.

Later that summer, Elizabeth
goes on a tour of Derbyshire,
where her aunt and uncle are

curious to see the Pemberley
estate. Not wanting to encounter
Darcy, she anxiously asks the
housekeeper if the master of the
house is in residence. She is
assured he is not, but the housekeeper goes on to praise Darcy
as a most kind and thoughtful
master. Elizabeth admires the
grandeur of the house, and
muses to herself that she might
have been mistress of so great

an estate. As she walks the grounds, she runs directly into Darcy, returning unexpectedly from a trip. Though he is astonished to see her, he recovers and displays great hospitality to her and the Gardiners. Observing him at his own home, Elizabeth notes that Darcy radiates warmth and graciousness.

Alas, the pleasant time at Pemberley is cut short when

Elizabeth receives the gravest of news: her youngest sister Lydia has run off with none other than … Wickham! The initial hope is that he intends to make an honest woman of Lydia and secure a quick marriage in Scotland, but this hope is dashed when the couple is reported to be hiding in London. The disgrace of the whole Bennet family is at stake. Mr. Bennet and Mr. Gardiner go to London on a desperate search for the illicit pair, but all hope seems lost.

Then curious news comes that Mr. Wickham will agree to marry Lydia for a very modest sum. Mr. Bennet can only conclude that his brother-in-law has secretly offered a very hefty ransom to save the family name. Eventually Elizabeth discovers the real truth—it was Mr. Darcy

that offered the large sum of
money that appeased Wickham
and secured the lawful union,
ultimately saving her family
from ruin.

Mr. Bingley returns to the
Bennet estate and ask for Jane's
hand. Meanwhile, Elizabeth
receives a most astounding visit
from Lady Catherine de Bourgh,
who demands to know whether
Elizabeth is engaged to her

nephew. When Elizabeth reports she is not, Lady Catherine orders her to pledge that she will never accept an offer if he makes it—denouncing the potential match as highly unsuitable and detrimental to the noble family line. Elizabeth staunchly refuses to make such a promise. Soon Darcy makes his own visit, where he begs her to state whether her feelings have at all changed. She happily reports that her regard for him has completely altered. They both repent their own past natures which have kept them from one another, his of willful pride, hers in prejudging his character. The two are engaged, and the novel ends with a joyful double wedding of the two sensible Bennet sisters: now Mrs. Bingley and Mrs. Darcy.

Mansfield Park

(1814)

"We have a better guide in ourselves, if we would attend to it, than any other person can be."

—FANNY PRICE

MAJOR CHARACTERS

Fanny Price: The shy, often cowering, but ultimately virtuous heroine of the novel. Rescued from an impoverished home, she is taken in by her wealthy aunt and uncle at Mansfield Park— but is constantly reminded of her lowly station.

Sir Thomas Bertram: Fanny's stern but sometimes tender uncle—master of Mansfield Park as well as a plantation in the West Indies.

Edmund Bertram: The kind-hearted second son of Sir Thomas, his aspiration is to become a clergyman.

Maria and Julia Bertram:

Edmund's shallow, spoiled sisters.

Henry and Mary Crawford:

The brother and sister of the local vicar's wife, they have come from London to stay near Mansfield.

THE STORY

The novel opens with a bit of family history: Years ago, a gentlewoman with a modest income made a very advantageous match by marrying Sir Thomas Bertram, baronet of Mansfield Park. But Lady Bertram's two sisters didn't fare as well. One made a much more humble yet respectable marriage with a vicar and became

Mrs. Norris, and the other made a disastrous choice in marrying a low-ranked sailor with a penchant for drinking—a decision that cut her off from her family. Now, years later, faced with a ninth pregnancy and her husband's dwindling income, a desperate Mrs. Price pleads for her sisters' help. Sir Thomas and Lady Bertram offer to take in the eldest Price daughter, raising her alongside their two sons and two daughters. However, they are clear that Fanny must never consider herself a *Miss Bertram*, and are always mindful of how fortunate she is to receive such generosity. Mrs. Norris, who thinks herself the model for Christian charity, is especially firm on insisting that Fanny never think too well of herself, or rise above her station.

Fanny comes to Mansfield when she is ten years old—a timid girl who withers next to her cousins Maria and Julia. Edmund, the second Bertram son who is meant for the church, is the only one who is friendly to his poor relation. He soothes Fanny's homesickness upon her arrival, and encourages her to write to her favorite brother, William.

The story advances a few years, where an eighteen-year-old Fanny has settled in to her life at Mansfield. She is well-provided for, yet she is generally considered to be invisible in the household. Though Maria and Julia have been her childhood companions, the social boundaries are firm: the sisters are "out" in society, while Fanny can only listen to reports of their various parties and balls. Much of Fanny's time is spent attending Lady Bertram, who is generally kind but oblivious to the wants and needs of others. Fanny's real pleasure is to ride her old gray pony. When he dies, no one except Edmund thinks to provide her with another horse. Fanny treasures Edmund's consistent kindness to her, and she

harbors tender feelings for
him.

The tranquility and stability
of Mansfield Park is disturbed
by the departure of Sir Thomas.
He must attend to his property
in Antigua, and expects to be
gone for at least a year. While
he is absent, chaos encroaches
upon Mansfield, propelled by
the arrival of Henry and Mary
Crawford. A brother and sister

pair, they have come from London and are staying with their older sister at the parsonage. Both are cosmopolitan and extremely charming, and they soon make friends with the inhabitants of Mansfield Park.

The Crawfords seem to revel in impropriety: Henry enjoys flirting with Maria and Julia, while Mary loves to rankle with her cynical and careless remarks. Maria, though engaged to the tiresome Mr. Rushworth, finds it hard to resist Henry's attentions. Edmund, meanwhile, becomes entranced by Mary's wit and beauty. Fanny is pained when she sees Edmund's growing fascination with Mary, but she takes comfort that he remains her protector and advocate at Mansfield, which Edmund

demonstrates by insisting that
Fanny be included on a group
excursion to Mr. Rushworth's
estate. While there, Mary teases
Edmund about his choice of
profession, saying that distinc-
tion cannot be gained in the
church. Meanwhile, Maria
openly shows disdain for her
fiancé and continues to flirt
with Henry, to the point of
rivaling her own sister Julia for

his affection.

The scandalous behavior continues through the year, as the group entertains themselves by planning the performance of a racy play called *Lover's Vows*. The house is abuzz with the preparations: rehearsals, costume planning, and scenery making. Despite his initial reluctance to perform in the play, Edmund can't resist

Mary, and makes the forward gesture of casting himself as her lover. Only Fanny remains unwilling to participate in the vulgar behavior. Sir Thomas suddenly returns from his long stay in Antigua, and firmly puts a stop to the theatrics. With his arrival, order is somewhat restored to Mansfield—but trouble still brews as the Crawfords continue their influence.

Acting out of spite because Henry has not declared his love for her, Maria goes ahead and marries the wealthy but dull-witted Rushworth, and Julia accompanies her on the wedding journey. With the Bertram sisters gone, Fanny is able to blossom and gain a bit more attention and respect at Mansfield. Henry decides to court Fanny, at first just for pure amusement, but as time passes he finds himself genuinely in love. Fanny isn't tempted, as she remembers his roguish behavior with Maria and Julia. At the same time, Mary (mostly out of sheer boredom) tries to forge a friendship with Fanny—but Fanny remains cautious with both Crawfords.

Edmund continues to be consumed by his attraction to Mary

and ignores all indications of
their ultimate incompatibility.
While Mary proudly states that
"a large income is the best
recipe for happiness" and
boldly praises ambition,
Edmund still holds out hope
that she may accept the lot of
becoming a clergyman's wife.
He confides in Fanny over his
stymied courtship, which
leaves Fanny flustered with her

powerful feelings for him.

Fanny's beloved brother, William, now a mid-shipman in the Navy, pays a visit to Mansfield. During his stay, Sir Thomas indulges Fanny by throwing a ball in her honor, where it's noticed that she has developed into a very pretty woman. Later, Henry facilitates a promotion for William to the rank of lieutenant, a favor that he is sure will make Fanny beholden to him. He proposes, but she baffles everyone, particularly Sir Thomas, by refusing. Though Sir Thomas is often tender to his niece, in this case he judges her harshly. Fanny's rejection of so advantageous a match seems like obstinate behavior on her part, and he suggests that she go back to her poor family in the hopes that time away from the "elegancies and luxuries of Mansfield Park, would bring her mind into a sober state" and make her reconsider her willful rejection of a marriage that would keep her in comfort.

Fanny travels home to Portsmouth, where she is shocked at the differences in living situation: the cramped conditions, the chaos of a home

with so many children, the
greasiness of the plates and sil-
verware. She soon longs for the
"elegance, propriety, regularity"
and harmony of Mansfield.
Henry pays a visit, making a
good impression with her
impoverished family. Still, he
leaves without any further
encouragement that he will win
her heart. Fanny waits for a letter from Edmund, nervous that

she'll hear the dreaded news
that he is engaged to Mary.
When the letter finally comes,
he reports that he is tortured by
Mary's "sentiments and expres-
sions" but that he cannot give
her up, writing "she is the only
woman in the world whom I
could ever think of as a wife."
Fanny is angry that he is
blinded by love, and mourns
that he will marry a woman so

ill-suited to his character.

Fanny receives another letter—this time from Mary. The missive confirms the writer's cold-blooded nature, as she glibly refers to the grave illness of Edmund's older brother, Tom. Mary goes on to joke that his death would mean that Edmund could inherit the baronetcy, a prospect that would be extremely pleasing to her.

A most shocking and sur-
prising event hastens Fanny's
return to Mansfield: Maria has
left Rushworth and run off
with Henry, leaving everyone in
a state of grief over her ruin.
Once Fanny arrives, Edmund
reveals that he has broken with
Mary, and tells how he finally
realized her true character. He
was stunned when Mary made
light of her brother's seduction

of a married woman. She was
only sorry that Henry and
Maria had been caught, but did
not find fault in the deed itself.
Very soon after he relays this
news, Edmund comes to his
senses and declares his love for
Fanny. He has loved, guided,
and protected her all along, and
she has been the beacon of all
goodness. The novel ends with
Sir Thomas giving the blessing

for their marriage, rejoicing that Fanny is now his daughter. Peace and tranquility has been truly, blissfully restored to Mansfield Park. Alas, there is just a breath of sinister undercurrent with this joyous conclusion, upon remembering that the Eden-like estate is supported by the proceeds of Sir Thomas' sugar plantation in the Caribbean—a place that

has no similar hope for order,
peace, or a happy ending.

Emma

(1816)

"*The real evils indeed of Emma's situation were the power of having rather too much her own way, and a disposition to feel a little too well of herself.*"

MAJOR CHARACTERS

Emma Woodhouse: The younger daughter of a wealthy landowner, she thrives on her role of managing not only her father's estate of Hartfield, but many of the social affairs in the village.

Mr. George Knightley: The owner of the nearby estate of Donwell Abbey and Emma's trusted friend. In his late thirties, he is a man of good sense and sound judgment.

Harriet Smith: A pleasant but slow-witted girl who Emma takes on as her protégé.

Frank Churchill: A foppish yet charming young man who piques Emma's interest.

Mrs. Weston: Emma's former governess and now her closest confidante. Mrs. Weston's recent marriage has made her Frank's stepmother.

Jane Fairfax: An orphan who comes to the village to stay with

her grandmother and aunt, she
is highly regarded for her elegance and reserve.

THE STORY

Twenty-year-old Emma Woodhouse is described as "handsome, clever, and rich, with a
comfortable home and happy
disposition." Because of her
mother's long-ago death and
her elder sister's marriage, she

is very much the mistress of the house. She dotes on her elderly, doddering father, and has enjoyed the companionship of her former governess and now treasured friend, Miss Taylor. At the beginning of the story, Miss Taylor (now Mrs. Weston) is wed, leaving Emma to search for another companion to fill much of her time—and she finds her in Harriet Smith, a resident of the local boarding school. Harriet is a sweet, pretty girl, but a hopeless simpleton. Moreover, she is of questionable parentage, which narrows her chances for marrying well.

Herself determined not to marry, Emma nevertheless delights in orchestrating the love life of her newfound friend. Harriet receives an offer of marriage from Robert Martin, a farmer who seems to have a sincere affection for her, but Emma encourages Harriet to refuse him and set her sights higher. Mr. Knightley, Emma's brother-in-law and longtime family friend, scolds Emma for her meddling. She may have foiled Harriet's best chance for a suitable and happy marriage. Emma heartily disagrees, say-

ing that Harriet has the potential for becoming a gentle-
woman, and feels quite sure
that the vicar Mr. Elton will
soon be proposing to Harriet.
But Emma is mortified to discover that *she* is the object of
Mr. Elton's passions, not Harriet. Emma tells Mr. Elton that
there has been a misunder-
standing—and he scoffs at the
idea that he would ever marry

someone of Harriet's station.

News comes that there will be two visitors to the village of Highbury. One visitor intrigues Emma, the other she dreads. The first is Frank Churchill, Mr. Weston's son from his first marriage, who will be staying at his father's home. Mr. Weston was widowed when Frank was just a baby, and he reluctantly entrusted his son to the care of

his rich in-laws, the Churchills.
On the condition that Frank
take their surname, the
Churchills have provided him
with a very privileged upbring-
ing and Frank is now a handsome young man who stands to
inherit their fortune. Everyone
in the village is looking forward
to meeting Mr. Weston's son.
Mr. Knightley is the only one
who has reservations about this

"trifling, silly fellow."

Jane Fairfax is the other visitor. She and Frank share similar histories: they have both been very lucky to have been taken under the wing of wealthy families. Jane's future, however, does not look as rosy. She had been orphaned as a little girl and been provided for by Colonel Campbell, who had known Jane's father in the war.

Campbell took on his comrade's orphan, affording her every comfort and generally making her part of his family. But because he had children of his own, there could be no expectation that he would continue to support her after she came of age. Now that Jane is nearing the age of independence, she resigns to come to Highbury and stay with her

poor relations, the Mrs. and
Miss Bates—knowing that her
likely future will be to find a
station as a governess. Though
Emma pities Jane's fate, she
nevertheless dislikes her. She
has known Jane since they were
girls, and she has always found
in her a "coldness and reserve"
that impeded any intimate
friendship. Knightley, percep-
tive as ever, knows that Emma

is truly jealous of Jane's elegance and talents.

Emma meets Frank Churchill, and has a very good opinion of him. But she is slightly disillusioned when she hears that he has taken a trip to London simply to get his hair cut—a foolish extravagance by anyone's measure. Still, she is charmed by his attentions at a local dance, where they share

fun in their mutual gentle
mockery of Jane.

Everyone is speculating on
who may have sent Jane a mysterious present of a pianoforte.
Frank laughingly says that it
must be a secret admirer.
Meanwhile, Mrs. Weston pre-
dicts that Mr. Knightley will
make Jane an offer. Emma
scoffs at this notion, saying
that her good friend Mr.

Knightley has no intention of marrying. But when Knightley gallantly orders a carriage to take Jane home, Emma is left to wonder whether Mr. Knightley truly intends to stay a bachelor.

Frank is briefly called away to the Churchills. On his departure Emma senses that there is a burgeoning attraction between them, yet she keeps her steadfast belief that she will never marry and resolves to encourage his affections toward Harriet upon his return. Mr. Elton (having departed the village after Emma's rejection) comes back with a new wife. Mrs. Elton proves to be an insufferable, superficial woman—and Emma is surprised to see that the reserved Jane and the bombastic Mrs. Elton soon become constant companions.

Another big dance is organized, and Emma is very pleased to see Mr. Knightley making the kind gesture of dancing with Harriet after she is cruelly snubbed by Mr. and Mrs. Elton. The next day, Emma is astonished to see Harriet leaning on the arm of Frank Churchill— recovering from a most harrowing event. Frank had just gallantly rescued her from a band of gypsies. Soon after, Harriet tells Emma that she has fallen in love with a man superior to her station, and Emma assumes that it must be Frank Churchill. Meanwhile, Mr. Knightley's dislike of Frank deepens, suspecting that Frank is somehow attached to Jane, while he shamelessly flirts with Emma. Once again, Emma dismisses Mr. Knightley's theories.

Mr. Knightley invites everyone to his estate for a picnic.
There Frank and Emma share
in playful banter. Encouraged by
Frank's teasing repartee, Emma
openly mocks Miss Bates for her
tiresome conversation. Mr.
Knightley takes her aside and
chides her for her rudeness.
Knowing that she has lost the
good opinion of Mr. Knightley
hurts Emma deeply.

Frank's rich aunt dies—and in just a few days the mystery is revealed: He has been secretly engaged to Jane for many months (he was also the benefactor of the pianoforte). His attentions to Emma were just a ruse to distract gossipers from the true object of his affection. Now that his disapproving aunt can no longer impede the union, he is free to marry. Mrs.

Weston delivers this remarkable news to Emma, while expressing regret that Emma may have been misled by his behavior. Emma assures her she was never seriously attached to Frank, but she worries this news may be another disappointment for Harriet.

There is yet another revelation: Harriet does not care for Frank, but rather Mr. Knight-

ley. Emma is extremely upset
upon hearing this admission,
and she wonders to herself
why she should react so
strongly. Emma realizes she
truly loves Mr. Knightley, and
that he should marry no one
but her. But she is pained
because she believes Mr.
Knightley returns Harriet's
affections—until the final mis-
understanding is resolved: It is

Emma that Mr. Knightley truly loves. At the end of the novel, Robert Martin renews his proposal to Harriet, and this time is accepted. And Knightley and Emma wed, whereby, "the wishes, the hopes, the confidence, the predictions of the small band of true friends who witnessed the ceremony, were fully answered in the perfect happiness of the union."

Northanger Abbey

"No one who had ever seen
Catherine Morland in her
infancy would have supposed
her born to be an heroine."

MAJOR CHARACTERS

Catherine Morland: A naive seventeen-year-old daughter of a parson who has come to Bath with family friends.

Isabella Thorpe: Catherine's best friend upon her arrival at

Bath. Her main interests are gossip and fashion.

John Thorpe: Isabella's brother, an arrogant bore who takes an interest in Catherine.

James Morland: Catherine's mild-mannered brother and a student at Oxford.

Henry and Eleanor Tilney: A brother and sister who display good sense, intelligence, and wit.

Captain Frederick Tilney:
Henry and Eleanor's older
brother, who often trifles with
women's affections.

General Tilney: Henry and
Eleanor's father—an imposing
figure who is the master of
Northanger Abbey.

THE STORY

From the first line of the novel, our heroine, Catherine Morland, is described as not possessing "heroine" qualities. She is young, without many accomplishments, and by her mother's account, "*almost* pretty." But to her credit, "her heart was affectionate; her disposition cheerful and open, without conceit or affectation of any kind." At age seventeen, she is invited to accompany family friends to the resort town of Bath, giving her the opportunity to leave her small village and get out among society. At one of the first balls she attends, Catherine meets a very agreeable gentleman who engages her in witty banter: It is Henry Tilney, a twenty-six-year-old clergyman, who comes "from a very respectable family in Gloucestershire."

Catherine hopes to see more of Henry, but she doesn't encounter him again for quite some time. Meanwhile, she strikes up a great friendship with Isabella Thorpe, a lively young woman who loves to gossip and talk about hats and ribbons. Soon Isabella and Catherine are inseparable. One common interest they share is reading Gothic novels: popular, melodramatic romances that usually feature a heroine in distress, often trapped in a mysterious castle. Another tie that binds them is that Isabella's brother John and Catherine's brother James are good friends at Oxford. When the young men make a visit to Bath, Catherine discovers that John

Thorpe is a bit of a "rattle"—a man who prattles on without having anything much to say. Catherine endures his cloddish comments, but certainly doesn't encourage his affections. Nevertheless, John takes an immediate liking to her.

Happily for Catherine, she finally sees Henry Tilney again at another dance—this time with his sister. Miss Eleanor

Tilney has "a very agreeable countenance," just like her brother. Catherine dances with the delightful Henry again, and also befriends Eleanor. The three of them make plans to meet the next day for a country walk. Catherine arrives at the appointed time, but Henry and Eleanor do not come. As she continues to wait, John Thorpe persuades her to take a ride in

his carriage. She reluctantly
agrees—but as soon as John
speeds up the horses, she spots
the Tilneys rounding the cor-
ner, and they look at her quizzi-
cally. She begs John to stop and
let her off but he merely laughs
and continues on. Catherine is
extremely vexed—not only that
she is trapped on a carriage
with an oafish man, but that the
Tilneys might think she aban-

doned them in favor of John Thorpe's company. The next day she endeavors to apologize and explain to Henry and Eleanor, and soon they are a merry trio of friends once again.

Since Catherine met the Tilneys, Isabella has been feeling a bit slighted, and tries in vain to persuade Catherine to jilt her new friends in favor of spending time with her and John. Catherine is annoyed to discover that John means to propose to her, and implores Isabella to tell him that she has no interest. Meanwhile, Isabella becomes engaged to Catherine's brother James. Isabella is elated that she and Catherine will be sisters-in-law—but Isabella's joy seems a bit tempered when she discovers that James' income is much less than she thought. Soon Isabella is openly flirting with Henry and Eleanor's older brother, Captain Frederick Tilney. Fearing that her beloved brother's engagement is in jeopardy, Catherine asks Henry if he can encourage Captain Tilney to leave Bath so that he isn't a temptation to Isabella. But Henry rightfully states that if Isabella is really in love with James, then another man can pose no threat.

General Tilney, Henry and Eleanor's father, asks Catherine to accompany them to the Tilney family home of Northanger Abbey. Since making her acquaintance, General Tilney has been very amiable toward Catherine, and this invitation to the Abbey is like a dream come true for her. On the journey, Catherine tells Henry that she has heard such wonderful things about his family's estate. Henry gently teases her about "gloomy chambers" and, knowing her love for Gothic novels, suggests that she might discover a secret passageway during a violent storm, and happen upon a mysterious manuscript. She is surprised

when Northanger Abbey turns
out to be not a dark, dank castle
but rather a bright, pleasant
house. Yet she cannot help but
be influenced by Henry's yarn,
and her imagination runs wild
on her first night at Northanger, resulting in a highly
comic scene. With wind blow-
ing, rain pelting against the
windows, and heart beating
fast, she comes across a con-

cealed chest of drawers with papers stashed in its cavities. She expects to find that enigmatic manuscript that Henry had suggested, but it is revealed to be . . . a long account of the laundry inventory.

In the daylight, the Abbey is more beautiful and stately than she imagined, with grounds of woody hills and old trees. Upon hearing more of the family's history, Catherine again lets her imagination run loose, unduly influenced by her devotion to Gothic novels. When Eleanor tells the story of her mother's death of a sudden illness almost a decade ago, Catherine forms a theory that their mother was actually killed by General Tilney. She gets carried away with this speculation, and makes the mistake of shar-

ing it with Henry. He firmly dis-
abuses her of her fantastic
notions, and she runs off in
tears of shame. She despairs
that he should think ill of her,
and wonders if his good opinion can be won again. But the
next day she finds Henry just as
affable as ever. She realizes her
folly in being so consumed by
these silly novels and promises
herself that she'll act with the

"greatest good sense" in the future.

During her stay at Northanger Abbey, Catherine gets a letter from her brother, saying that his engagement to Isabella has been called off, and suggesting that Captain Tilney is the cause. Henry and Eleanor wait to hear of any news from their brother about the affair. In the meantime, Catherine is delighted that Henry has invited her and Eleanor to visit his parsonage at Woodston. Henry leaves for a few days to prepare the house for them, while General Tilney goes to London for business. She soon receives a letter from Isabella, telling her that James is the only man she has loved, and that Captain Tilney is the "greatest coxcomb I ever saw, and amazingly disagreeable." Catherine can read between the lines: Captain Tilney has been a cad, and has made Isabella no promises after he tempted her out of her engagement. Isabella goes on to ask Catherine to act on her behalf and petition her brother to renew his offer of marriage. Catherine is disgusted after reading the letter, and sees her friend for the vain, self-serving, manipulative person she truly is. Catherine chooses not to answer the letter—her silence will be enough to indicate her disapproval and disillusion.

General Tilney returns from London, and inexplicably casts Catherine out of Northanger, ordering a carriage to take her away the next morning. There is no explanation for such a complete change in his demeanor. Just a few days before, the general was paying her compliments and alluding to Henry's attachment to her. What could account for such an outrageous dismissal? She continues to be dumbfounded when she arrives home, and is bereaved that she has lost such treasured friendships. But soon Henry arrives to explain everything. It turns out that, on a whim, John Thorpe had told a bit of a fib to General Tilney, saying that Catherine had a large fortune. This explains the general's warm hospitality and his encouragement of her relationship with Henry. John Thorpe then acted out of revenge (partly because of Catherine's rejection of his affections and partly because she refused to aid in reconciling his sister's engagement) and he later admitted his fib to the general, adding that Catherine was a woman of no social standing at all. This had caused the general to order Catherine's expulsion from his home. Henry castigated his father for his egregious behavior, and hurried to her side as soon as he could. Henry assures Catherine of his true affections, and asks for her hand in marriage.

All ends in happiness: Eleanor makes a very favorable marriage to a Lord, and General Tilney eventually convinces himself that Catherine has suitable connections after all. Henry and Catherine wed, and the couple is reinstated to Northanger Abbey. Catherine is most certainly cured of her follys: no longer allowing her-

self to be carried away by false
friends or the high drama of
ridiculous novels.

Persuasion

"All the privilege I claim for my
own sex...is that of loving longest
...when hope is gone."

—ANNE ELLIOT

MAJOR CHARACTERS

Anne Elliot: The second daughter of the Elliot clan and protagonist of the novel.

Frederick Wentworth: A navy captain who has returned from a long stint at sea.

Lady Russell: A close friend of
the Elliot family who serves as
a maternal advisor for Anne.

Sir Walter Elliot: A vain, self-
important baronet, and patri-
arch of the Elliot family.

Mary Elliot Musgrove: Anne's
younger sister, who has married into the Musgrove family.

Louisa Musgrove: Mary's sister-in-law and potential love interest of Wentworth's.

William Elliot: Anne's estranged cousin and heir-presumptive to the Elliot estate.

Mrs. Smith: An impoverished widow and Anne's girlhood friend.

THE STORY

Anne Elliott is sensitive, clever, and practical—qualities that go largely unnoticed by her family. Her beloved mother died thirteen years before, leaving her with a father and two sisters who at best are benignly neglectful of Anne, and at worst, openly condescending. Her father, Sir Walter Elliott, is a narcissist whose extravagance has overextended the family's fortune, forcing him to cut back on expenses and rent out the family home. The arrangements are made for Kellynch-Hall to be let to an Admiral and Mrs. Croft. The discovery that Mrs. Croft is the sister of one Captain Frederick Wentworth brings up painful memories for Anne. Almost a decade before, she and Wentworth had fallen

in love and had an understanding that they would marry. But
she had been persuaded to
release herself from the
engagement by her most
trusted confidante and mother
figure, Lady Russell, who
thought Wentworth lacking in
proper profession and connections. Anne has bitterly regret-
ted giving him up, and as a
result she has lost much of the

bloom of her youth—resigning herself to a life of spinsterhood at the age of twenty-seven.

Since the Crofts will be moving into Kellynch, the Elliott family will be dispersing: her father and eldest sister, Elizabeth, plan to stay in Bath. Accompanying them is the odious Mrs. Clay, a widow who, Anne suspects, has designs on her father. Anne is relieved to

remain in the neighborhood for
a few months—staying at
Uppercross Cottage with her
younger sister Mary, with the
understanding that she'll go to
Bath in a few months' time.
Mary is a chronic complainer
with a penchant for hypochon-
dria and treats Anne like a tiresome nursemaid. Still, Anne
enjoys her time among Mary's
family. Anne is highly regarded

by Mary's husband, Charles Musgrove, and his sisters, Louisa and Henrietta. News comes that Captain Wentworth will be visiting Mrs. Croft at Kellynch, and Anne braces herself for reuniting with her former paramour.

Their initial meeting is cool but civil. No one else in their social circle remembers their past connection—only vaguely recalling that the two had met years ago. Mary makes a careless remark, telling Anne that Wentworth found her "so altered he should not have known you again." Anne privately agonizes that Wentworth's "cold politeness and ceremonious grace were worse than anything."

Still, there are occasions when Anne is flustered by

Wentworth's subtle actions on her behalf: his help in releasing her from her young nephew's grasp, his hastening her into a carriage after a tiring walk. But it's clear to Anne that Wentworth has his eye on Louisa Musgrove, a young woman who boldly states, "once I have made up my mind, I have made it." Wentworth seems to admire her forthrightness—until she demonstrates it impetuously on a group stroll in the seaside town of Lyme. While walking along the sea wall, Louisa insists on jumping from a high ledge into Wentworth's arms. He tries to stop her, saying it too dangerous, but she will not be persuaded otherwise. She leaps, hits the stone path, and lies unconscious. Anne is the only one who remains com-

posed during the emergency.
Eventually it's determined that
Louisa has suffered a concus-
sion, and with proper rest she'll
make a recovery. Wentworth
reproaches himself for the acci-
dent, but is reminded of Anne's
capable nature.

Anne joins her family in
Bath—and when she arrives
she learns that her father has
made amends with his nephew

and the future heir of Kellynch, Mr. William Elliot. Years earlier, William had married a rich woman of inferior birth, and had inexplicably fallen out of communication with his uncle and Sir Walter had felt extremely put out. Now, a decade later, Mr. Elliot is recently widowed, and all seems to be forgiven. In fact, everyone seems absolutely delighted with this prodigal relation. Anne also finds him agreeable, with charming manners—and likes him even more when she discovers they share a concern over Mrs. Clay's influence on Sir Walter. Anne senses her cousin's growing affection for her. Lady Russell praises the potential match, encouraging Anne to accept him if he makes her an offer.

The marriage would secure Anne as mistress of Kellynch, and Lady Russell would delight in seeing Anne elevated to her late mother's position. But Anne tells her she could never think of marrying him. Though she finds him generally pleasant, she feels they don't suit one another.

Meanwhile, Anne gets a letter from her sister Mary, who

has stayed at Uppercross to help nurse Louisa back to health. Mary reports the most extraordinary news: Louisa is now engaged to Captain Benwick, a poetic, sensitive soul who just a month before had seemed inconsolable over the loss of his late fiancée. Everyone is shocked by the news, partly because it seems like an odd match, but also because

many had assumed that Louisa
was already intended for Wentworth. Admiral Croft reports
that Wentworth does not act
like a spurned suitor—on the
contrary, he seems genuinely
happy about the match
between Louisa and his friend.
Upon hearing of Wentworth's
reaction to the engagement,
Anne can't help but feel just a
glimmer of hope for rekindling

their connection.

During her stay in Bath, Anne renews her friendship with an old school chum, Mrs. Smith, a penniless widow who has come to Bath to cure her rheumatic fever. Mrs. Smith assumes that Anne will soon be married to her cousin Mr. Elliot—but when Anne assures her that she is mistaken, Mrs. Smith is relieved, and feels free to speak the truth. Mrs. Smith's late husband was a close friend of Mr. Elliot's, and she has saved letters that expose his despicable motives. He is a scoundrel who married his first wife solely because of her extraordinary wealth. He had once scoffed at Sir Walter and his baronetcy, saying that he would sell the Elliot name and title for fifty pounds if anyone would have it. With his wife's fortune, Mr. Elliot led a lavish lifestyle and encouraged the Smiths to live well beyond their means. After her husband's death, Mrs. Smith was left in financial ruin, and desperately needed Mr. Elliot to act on her behalf to recover some assets. As executor of the will, Mr. Elliot refused to act accordingly, leaving her in dire financial straits. Mrs. Smith also explains his true reason for reconciling with the Elliots: He has reconsidered his thoughts on the value of a baronetcy, and is now intent on obtaining the title of Sir William. By recovering his influence with the family, he means to circumvent any hope of Mrs. Clay's becoming Lady Elliot (and possibly producing an heir). A marriage to

Anne would further cement his claims on the Kellynch Estate and his title as baronet.

Meanwhile, Wentworth has come to Bath, which affords many opportunities for him to have awkward, tentative encounters with Anne. At every meeting, Anne gets usurped by her cousin's attentions, which further thwart the pair. One morning, while everyone is

gathered in a parlor, Anne falls
into a meaningful conversation
with Wentworth's friend Captain Harville. They debate over
which sex is more constant in
their affections: men or
women. Harville asserts that
men "are the strongest, so are
our feelings; capable of bearing
most rough usage, and riding
out the heaviest weather." Anne
counters that women are capa-

ble of "loving longest . . . when
hope is gone"—a statement
that overwhelms her with emotion. Wentworth has overheard
this exchange, and abruptly
leaves the room. He returns to
fetch his gloves, then slips
Anne a note, which reads:
"You pierce my soul. I am half
agony, half hope. Tell me not that
I am too late, that such precious
feelings are gone for ever. I offer

myself to you again with a heart
even more your own, than when
you almost broke it eight years
and a half ago. Dare not say that
man forgets sooner than woman,
that his love has an earlier death.
I have loved none but you."

The two blissfully come
together—and Wentworth
admits to having "angry pride"
when they met at Uppercross—
and of the folly of his passing

interest in Louisa. Upon hearing of Anne and Wentworth's engagement, Mr. Elliot is shocked that his plans are foiled but consoles himself by running off with Mrs. Clay to London. Wentworth makes amends with Lady Russell over her earlier influence on Anne, and helps Mrs. Smith regain some of her property. Though Austen satisfies her readers

with a happy ending, there is
also a sense of impending dan-
ger in the last paragraph of the
novel: that as a sailor's wife,
Anne is all tenderness, but that
the "dread of a future war [was]
all that could dim her sun-
shine."

ART CREDITS